Love, Lie and ¦
Daniell

Love, Lie and Regret.
A second chance short story.

Danielle Jacks

Love, Life and Regret.

Love is a complex four letter word.

Life is the path we choose for ourselves, but can come with sacrifices.

Regret; when love and life don't quite fit.

Love, life, and regret is a story of second chances when marriage doesn't mean happily ever after.

Chapter One
Kristie

Monday

"Do you know why I've called this meeting today?" Mr Masters, the executive director, says. He gives me his usual stern look that puts my nerves on edge.

I keep my back straight, crossing my legs. Keeping Mr Masters happy makes my job as a hotel manager easier, so whatever he wants, I need to deliver. "Foundations Manor is doing well in the elegance hotel range. The latest figures show an increase in revenue, and although the new vegetable garden isn't fully constructed, we've had a good supply of local produce from the farms on the outskirts of Manchester." I say, aiming to please, although not everything is running smoothly.

"I'm proud of the work you've done. The hotel has been doing great, and that's why it's been chosen for a documentary about some of England's luxury escapes."

I let out the breath I'd been holding. I'm so relieved it's good news. "That's excellent. I'm ready for a challenge." I smile brightly.

I love the *Luxury Escapes* series, and it would be great for business if the hotel made it onto the show.

"I knew you'd be up to the task. We're going to need an up-to-date CRB check and a full disclosure of any hidden skeletons that might shadow a dark cloud on the hotel." A hint of a smile plays on his lips for the first time since I've known him, and I'm thrilled.

"There's nothing to worry about. I don't have a criminal record, obviously."

Excitement flutters in my stomach. This is a big deal. If it goes well, I'll be one of the faces of the company. My job will be as secure as it can be, or I might be able to apply for a promotion.

"And your personal life is straightforward? Your mum and dad are happily married? No axe murderer or secret love child?" He actually laughs at his own joke. I didn't even know he had a sense of humour.

"No. My parents are retired, and I have no children." My life isn't glamorous, but I've sacrificed a lot to get where I am. I gave up my home in Scotland, leaving my family behind. The pit of my stomach fills with dread. "I'm technically married, but we're separated. Freddie won't cause any problems." The excitement I felt fizzles into sadness I don't want to feel. Freddie's more likely to shut the door in anyone's face if they come snooping around. He's a traditional man who likes to keep his personal life private.

"It's good he won't be a problem, but if you tie off the loose ends, it'll be even better. Then we won't have to worry about it, will we?"

"Get a divorce?" I ask slowly as the information comes together in my mind.

"Yes. I'm giving you the week off to get this sorted. Your assistant manager can hold down the fort until you get back, or if you prefer, you can mail him the papers, but I want this taking care of ASAP."

There's no way Freddie would sign the divorce papers if I sent them in the post, even if I called him. Actually, I'd be lucky if he didn't block my number and return the letter as ash. "We don't talk anymore, but I can assure you he isn't a problem. He won't say a word to any reporters." Or maybe not even me. We didn't leave things on good terms.

"You're one of my best managers. I'm sure you can handle this." He stands, ready to leave, as I mumble unintelligent sounds, trying to come up with an excuse not to go.

"Okay," I finally say as he reaches the door. I'm not going to win this argument, so I don't have a choice. My life's work is invested in the hotel industry, and I don't want to lose this opportunity. He leaves the room, and I slump down into the chair.

Freddie never wanted me to take the first manager's job in Scotland, so he's not going to be happy he needs to help my career now. I find his social media account, which is set to private. The picture of Loch Venachar is unmistakable. Our small, quaint wedding set against the beautiful stretch of water flashes through my mind. It was a magical day. Freddie's face when I told him I was moving to Edinburgh sours my memory, and the let-down in his features when I said I was leaving the country was even worse. When I asked him to come with me, he made it clear he wasn't willing to up his life for a job opportunity. What we had together wasn't perfect, but I do miss him. I need to take care of this quickly, then I'll never have to disappoint him again.

"Ms Butler, you wanted to see me?" Jody, one of my new recruits, says. I raise my eyes to take in her appearance. The wetness of her hair is a mockery in itself, and I fight back a disapproving frown.

"Yes. Come in." I straighten down my skirt and sit up correctly in my chair.

"Okay." Jody offers a weak smile as she

stumbles into my office.

"How do you think your first two weeks have gone?" I give her a chance to redeem herself, although I doubt this is going to end well.

"I've enjoyed working with the team. I've grasped how to make a bed."

"What about your code of conduct?" My jaw tightens. I hope I'm not going to have to spell this out for her.

"I haven't spoken to many guests, but I'm always polite."

I sigh heavily. This is the worst part of my job, but it has to be done. "I've had reports of you using the hotel guests' facilities."

"I was on a break and my hair didn't look very professional," she says, trying to justify herself. I don't think she means to be rude, but her excuse is not good enough.

"The truth is, you just don't fit in at Foundations Manor. I need people who respect the brand and are focused on delivering an excellent service."

"So you're letting me go?" Her bottom lip quivers, and I hold back my frustration. I hate criers, so I try another approach.

"If you want to work in the hospitality sector, you need to strive for gold standard customer service skills. I gave you a chance because you seemed eager to learn, even though your CV was less than impressive."

"All I did was wash my hair," she says, like she's not grasping it's a big deal.

"You also helped yourself to the minibar," I say, not as friendly as before.

"It was a few chocolates. I could pay for them." She digs around in her pocket.

"I'm sorry. This isn't working out, so I'm going to have to let you go. Collect your belongings and leave the premises." I pick up my pen and make a note on my pad, hoping she won't make this anymore torturous than it has to be.

She lingers in the doorway for a few seconds

before exiting. About ten minutes later, Shannon, my deputy manager and best friend, enters my office.

"Hi. I've had to fill the vases with artificial flowers, but I don't think Mr Masters noticed," Shannon says.

I rub my hands over my eyes. "That's the least of my worries, but I'm glad to see you."

"Mr Masters' visit wasn't very long. What did he want?" Shannon approaches the window. I swivel my chair around to face her.

"*Luxury Escapes*, the TV show we sometimes watch on Sunday nights, is going to do a feature on the hotel. We're going to be on TV," I say, but my excitement is clouded by the idea of seeing my ex again.

"Oh, that sounds exciting." She rubs her palms together. "Will we have speaking parts?"

"I think they'll follow us around on normal working days."

"I thought you'd be more enthusiastic about this. Why don't you seem more upbeat?"

"The show sounds like a good opportunity." I sigh heavily.

"Then what's the glum face for?" She leans her back against the glass.

"Mr Masters asked if there was anything in my personal life that a reporter could use for bad press."

"You're almost a saint so there's no problem there." She draws an imaginary halo on her head, and I fight back a laugh. I wish I could argue, but she's right. I'm almost squeaky clean, except for the fact I'm still married. I haven't been with anyone else, so even that isn't scandalous.

"I know, but he told me I need to resolve my relationship with Freddie and file for divorce. He wants it done before we start filming."

"Why are you worried about this? You've been separated for a year. Fill out the forms and post them to him."

I left Scotland about a year ago, but my marriage was already on the rocks when I took the management job in Edinburgh. The long hours meant I slept at the hotel more than at home.

"Freddie's old school. If I want the divorce to go through without any hitches, I'll have to go deliver the papers personally." An unsettling feeling washes over me. Divorce is so final. Going to Scotland will give me the closure I probably need, but I'd be lying if I said I wasn't nervous about seeing him again.

"We have another problem to deal with first," Shannon says, looking out the window. I join her to see Jody sitting on the wall in her uniform.

I let out a groan. "That girl is trying my patience."

"Do you want me to deal with her?"

"No. I'll do it. You're going to have to hold down the fort while I'm away, so I think you should start with trying the chef's menu. I'll do the dirty work. I don't want you quitting on me while I'm away."

"It might be you that quits. Freddie's one good-looking guy. He looks like a beefy lumberjack from the pictures I've seen."

I don't talk about my ex much, but after a few drinks, I'd shown her some old photos of our wedding day. "He's a tree surgeon, and just because he has a beard, doesn't mean you have to drool all over him."

"It's my weakness." She fakes a damsel in distress pose.

"Yeah, mine too," I whisper with irritation as I'm heading out of my office. I might as well get this task over with so I can go to my room in the hotel and start packing my bags.

Chapter Two
Freddie

The tiny tabby cat holds onto my glove so tightly I can feel the claws piercing through my skin. "I've got you," I say to the little creature as I start to climb down the ladder.

"Poor thing must be frightened," Lisa, my friend and neighbour says.

"If only it would stop doing these stupid things."

"Tabs will learn in time. She's only five months old." She cradles her hand like she's holding the small kitten against her chest. I'll never understand her obsession with cats. When I reach the bottom of the ladder, the kitten jumps out of my hand and runs off into the garden. I fold down my ladder, ready to leave Lisa's house. She's a nice woman, but there are better things for me to be doing with my time.

"I should be on my way," I say, giving her a warm smile.

"Thank you for coming to my rescue yet

again, Freddie. Let me cook you dinner to show my appreciation." She bats her eyelashes.

"You're more than welcome, but no thanks is needed. I'm happy to help when you have a problem. I'm sorry to cut my visit short, but I've got things to do. I'll see you soon," I say, trying to shut the conversation down. "Call me if you need me," I add, hoping I'm not coming across as rude. I never accept any of her offers for dinner, but she never seems to grasp I'm happy with my own company.

"Don't you think it's time you moved on? Kristie left Scotland months ago." She looks hopeful I'll change my mind, but it just causes me pain.

"It's over a year, but who's counting?" I say bitterly.

At first, I didn't date because I held onto the hope Kristie would come back. When she started working in Edinburgh, I knew the communication between us was dwindling, but I never expected her to move to England. We'd survived high school together and got married. I thought that meant we'd be together for life. She asked me to go with her, but I was too stubborn to consider it. She didn't call, and I was too proud to make the first move. I don't date because, in my eyes, I'm married, even if my wife isn't around. I've been celibate for so long, I'm surprised my dick hasn't fallen off.

"I could help you forget about her," Lisa says, biting her lip. Her husband died a few years ago, so I try to be friendly, although I'm not interested in starting anything romantic with her. She's a good-looking woman, but I'm not available.

"I'm doing okay on my own." My meals for one and sleeping on the couch are working out fine with me. I don't have anyone telling me I need to go to bed or how to look after my home.

"Maybe it's me that needs the company. I don't mean to sound pushy, but I get lonely in that big old house. I always imagined having children to liven the place up, but I guess it was never meant to be for Henry and me."

"I'm not searching for a family, Lisa. You deserve someone better. Someone who can give you all the things you need."

"If I'm being honest, it's the children I want more than a new husband. Henry was everything to me, and I could never fully replace him with someone else."

"What are you saying?" I must be asking for punishment today, especially if this proposition is going where I think it is.

"I'm offering no strings attached fun, or whatever you're willing to give."

If things were different, maybe I'd be interested. With her blonde hair, big boobs, and beautiful eyes, she's a catch for the right man. But she's not Kristie. Nobody has ever compared to her. Her rich brown hair and hazel eyes drew me in from the first time I saw her in high school. It doesn't matter how much time has passed; I meant what I said on our wedding day. I'm unavailable, both emotionally and physically, although I don't want to hurt Lisa's feelings. I can't accept that Kristie's gone forever until she tells me herself. "I'm sorry. I just can't." I shake my head.

"Before you say no, think about what I'm offering. There's no need for us both to be miserable when we could help each other fill some of the voids."

I nod, wanting to get away from this conversation before I say something stupid. Deep down, Lisa knows I'm still in love with my wife, even if it is misguided. I pick up the ladder and quickly get out of there.

What is wrong with me? A perfectly good woman is offering me some company, and I made her practically throw herself at my feet. I made her sound desperate and a little crazy, which wasn't my intention. I've always known Lisa wants a child, but I'm not a sperm donor.

I attach my ladder to my truck and make a hasty exit without looking back. I drive to the woodland area my team is working at today and park up. The chainsaw's heavy, but I'm used to the weight. I grab my helmet, goggles, and equipment, ready to get back to work. Lisa's calls have gotten more frequent recently, but it's probably because of the new feline. I enjoy my job, but I never thought I'd be climbing trees to rescue cats as a hobby.

"We're laying the new overhead electrical cable soon," Scott says, giving me the evil eye. He gets grumpy when we're behind schedule.

"Sorry I'm late. Lisa needed help with that damn kitten again," I say as I get closer.

"I don't think it's the kitten she wants help with." He gives me a knowing look.

"She's harmless enough." I shrug off his comment.

Once I have my harness on, I climb up the tree. The work is already marked out and the hours pass quickly. I guzzle down my water when we're finished, load some fire logs onto my truck, and pack up my things for the day.

The second I get home, I know something's amiss. The door's slightly ajar, and it looks like the mud has been swept off my front doorstep that I'd left for months. The only person who ever cared about the appearance of the lodge was Kristie, but that can't be right. *Why would she be here?*

I'm slow to unload my things from the bed of the truck while I collect my thoughts. What a strange day I'm having. Lisa has never turned up at my house, so I doubt it's her inside. I'm pretty sure my mother wouldn't clean up, so I'm running out of ideas as to who it could be. I take off my muddy boots and put them into the shoebox I made on the front decking.

I edge open the door and walk inside. The rattling of pots in the kitchen and the smell of a home-cooked meal should unnerve me, but my gut is telling me this isn't Lisa. I poke my head around the door to confirm my suspicions. Kristie is right there in the kitchen, and I need a few minutes to think. Has she come home for good, or is there something else she wants? My nerves are instantly on edge. Instead of interrupting her, I go for the shower. I've had a busy day cutting down trees, so my aching muscles won't thank me for adding tension before soothing them. I leave my clothes outside the bathroom door and take my time getting washed. I dry off and wrap a towel around my waist.

Chapter Three
Kristie

Freddie's home, and I'm hiding out in our, I mean, *his* kitchen. This place still feels like home, even after all this time. I try to forget the warm feelings the lodge creates and focus my attention on the food.

Using the ricer, I grate the potatoes over the mincemeat before putting the dish back into the oven. I catch sight of Freddie dressed only in a towel. He's staring at me from the doorway with an intense stare. My gaze runs over his toned chest and down towards the only part of him that's covered up. A warm blush creeps over my face, but he's always been attractive, and it's nothing for me to be ashamed of.

He coughs loudly, bringing me out of my daze. Only Freddie affects me in this way, but I can't be distracted. Not when I need all my wits about me to convince him to sign the divorce papers.

"What are you doing here, Kristie?" he asks in a stern tone.

"No hello? I thought you'd be pleased to see me." I smile, feeling nervous and slightly awkward.

"You're trespassing on private land. I should call the police." He folds his arms across his chest.

"What's mine is yours, remember? Unless we get a divorce." I cringe. I'm usually more diplomatic than this.

"So, is that why you've come?" He steps into my space, towering over me.

I involuntarily lick my lips. The woodsy smell of his cologne lingers in my nostrils as I struggle not to melt into him. He smells so good.

I need to pull myself together and stop drooling. "Isn't it time for us to make our separation official? I'm not coming home." My voice squeaks out like a mouse.

"You're home now." He leans further into my space and I breathe him in.

"It was a slip of the tongue. I'm trying to

keep this pleasant. I'm living in Manchester now."

"Where's your heart?" His breath whispers along my ear, sending a shiver down to my core. I step back to put some distance between us.

Freddie and I never had a chemistry problem. Our difficulty was communicating outside the bedroom. He never asked me to stay or said he was proud of me. He made me feel like my ambition was a weakness instead of a strength, and it had made me miserable.

"Since when do you play games?"

He's always been honest with me. He never played with my feelings before.

"Are you scared you might like being here?" he challenges.

I clear my throat. "I've cooked a nice meal. I thought we could talk about this in a civil manner, like adults. I only have a small window of time before I need to get back."

"How long do you have?"

"I want to be back in Manchester as soon as possible."

"I didn't ask what you wanted. I asked how long you have off work?"

"A week."

"Okay." He leans back against the doorframe. The sly smile on his face tells me it isn't going to be that easy.

"So, we can have a nice evening to catch up," I say with scepticism. The confidence that usually holds strong in my voice is still missing. This is worse than a meeting with my boss.

"No. I have plans tonight, but we can get reacquainted later when it's convenient for us both."

"My train leaves at ten tonight."

"I thought you had a week."

"Yes, but I was hoping I wouldn't need it."

"Too bad, sweetheart, because I do."

He turns and starts to walk towards the bedroom, and I chase after him. "Don't walk away. We're not done."

"You've got that right."

When he reaches his underwear drawer, he drops the towel to the floor, leaving his bare ass on display.

"I haven't booked anywhere to stay and I've only brought a few things with me." I knew he'd be difficult. Damn. I should've told him I only had twenty-four hours.

He pulls on his boxers before turning to face me. "You've already said this is your home, so why would you need somewhere else to sleep?"

"I want a divorce, not to rekindle what we had." I throw my fist down by my side in frustration.

"If in a week you still want me to sign the papers, I will." He pulls on his jeans and tucks in his junk.

"If I stay in Scotland for seven days, you'll give me what I want?"

"If you stay in the lodge and play the role of my wife while you're here, then I'll give you what you want."

I sigh. "Fine."

He grabs a white t-shirt and pulls it over his head. I watch the material slip over his abs and hate the disappointment that rises within me when he finally covers up. "I'll be back around eleven." His voice is almost hostile, like he can't wait to get out of here. I don't understand why he wants me to stay for a week when he can't wait to get away from me.

"Shall I save you some food?"

"No, I'm good." He shakes his head.

I follow him to the door and watch him put his shoes on. "Have a good night," I say, even though I hope he doesn't have too much fun. I'd like him back early so we can talk.

"I will." He leans in and kisses my cheek. I'm not sure if it's out of old habits or to show me he's not being completely hostile towards me. Once he's gone, I touch the area.

Why did I let him do that?

Spending a week won't be so bad as long as

I keep my feelings in check. Foundations Manor is where I want to be, and it doesn't matter what Freddie says, I'm not changing my mind. If he wants to play house, then I'll have to show him how much better off he is without me.

Chapter Four
Freddie

"What are you doing here on a Monday night?" Lisa asks from her small table by the window. The Caterpillar and Leaf is the only pub around, so it's not a surprise to see her here.

"I thought I'd grab some food out." I hadn't completely thought my plan through when I left Kristie at the lodge, but I needed to get out of there and make sure she didn't leave while I gave myself time to think.

"Are you going to join me, or are you too independent for that?" Lisa asks, challenging me.

"I probably deserve that. I'm going to order a beer and a burger from the bar, then I'll be back. Can I get you anything?"

"A glass of red wine and a club sandwich would be great."

I nod and go to place our order. I take the seat opposite Lisa when I return with our drinks. "So what brings you here tonight?" I ask.

"This is my Monday night ritual. The real question is why you're here." She smiles, but it doesn't reach her eyes. I don't want any bad feelings between us. Our friendship is important to me, even if we want different things. Hopefully, we can share an unplanned meal together as friends and it won't mean anything more than that.

She's going to find out about Kristie sooner or later, so I might as well tell her now rather than dragging it out. "My wife showed up at the lodge." I brace myself for a telling off about letting Kristie walk back into my life.

"Oh. Does she want to get back together?" I don't miss the sadness in her voice, which wasn't what I expected. *Does Lisa like me more than she admits?*

I fake a laugh. "The opposite, actually."

"Aw, I'm sorry to hear that." She sounds sincere but just a little too happy about it for my liking.

I run my hands over my hair. "I guess it didn't feel final until now."

"It'll be good for you to move on. I know I've been pushy lately, but I do care about you. You've been a good friend, and I only want what's best for you." She rubs her ring finger over the rim of her wine glass and I wonder if she's thinking of Henry.

"Have you been on a date since Henry's death?" I grimace at my blunt tone.

"No, but I've signed up for a speed dating session on Friday. You should come."

I rub my hand over my face. "I don't know about that."

"If you don't put yourself out there, you'll never know what could've been."

I feel like she might be talking about herself, or even us, but I'm glad she's considering other options. Kristie showing up has put things in perspective. It's time to either put my heart on the line for us or let her go. When she left, I was arrogant enough to think she'd come back. By the time I'd realised my mistake, it was too late. I deserve this week to get closure on what happened and to show her what she's given up. By asking her to act like my wife, maybe I can figure out where I went wrong.

I enjoy talking with Lisa and eating pub food, which surprises me. The time passes quickly, and it's late once I've driven her home. The lodge is quiet when I arrive home, but I can sense it's not empty. The smell of vanilla and blackberries brings back memories of warm summer nights and having friends around, which I no longer do. Kristie's fancy wax melts were something I used to complain about, even though I didn't mind it as much as I made out. Now, the aroma reminds me of what I've lost, and it hurts.

I strip down to my boxers and brush my teeth in the bathroom sink. Her presence is also evident in here. Kristie's toothbrush is next to mine, and there's a pretty flower-shaped soap neatly placed over a folded flannel. I bring the items close to my nose and inhale deeply. Rosemary and peppermint is another reminder of Kristie and her rituals. I smile sadly but refuse to let the feeling deepen. I place the flannel and soap back on the side of the sink before exiting the bathroom.

Kristie's lying on the bed in her silky pink pyjamas and panda sleep mask. She looks cute, even as she snores softly. I walk around to the far side of the bed and it dips as I sit down. I take my watch off, abandoning it on the floor.

"What are you doing?" Kristie asks, lifting the mask from her eyes. The only light is coming from the small lamp I left on in the hallway.

"Going to bed," I say, sliding under the covers. I make sure I don't completely hide my chest. I didn't miss her lingering gaze earlier, and I don't plan on making this easy for her. I close my eyes, pretending I'm ready for sleep, although having her here isn't making me tired.

"Sorry. I didn't expect you to want to sleep in the bedroom. I thought you liked to sleep on the couch?" She wriggles on the bed. Even when we were together, I used to fall asleep in front of the TV. She used to moan if I didn't come to bed, which is ironic, because now she seems to feel the opposite.

"Yes, well things change," I lie. I probably only sleep in the bedroom half of the week.

"You'd better stay on your side," she huffs, snapping her mask back over her eyes.

"Fine by me," I say without the same conviction. I turn away from her, hoping I manage to drift off.

She tosses and turns in the bed while I stifle a laugh. I shouldn't be amused by her displeasure, but I am. This week I'm going to be myself. There is no point pretending to be something I'm not. I want her to stay for me. I know I got things wrong in the past, but I've been given this chance and I intend to use it. The problem is, I'm not sure my heart can take anymore breaking. I'm afraid I still might not be enough for her. I know she finds me attractive. My little stunt early made that obvious. So, if I can get her to open up to me, maybe we have a chance. I'm not going to bend over backwards to please her because that's not me, but if I can convince her she gave up something special, maybe I could have another chance at making her happy.

Chapter Five
Kristie

Tuesday

Waking up alone feels strange, even though I've been doing it for years. Freddie's side of the bed is cold. He's probably at work. I should be glad I don't have to spend every second with him, but I'd be lying if I didn't admit I'm disappointed he's gone. He demanded I stay the week, and he's only going to spend a few evenings with me. He doesn't have the kind of job where he has to go in every day, so he could've found someone to replace him. He could make more of an effort when he asked me to stay. He's already slipping into old patterns, which make me feel insecure. I did ask for a divorce and maybe this is what I deserve, but for once, I'd like him to consider what I want.

By lunchtime, I have the lodge cleaned from top to bottom and smelling like apple blossom. I turn off my old wax melt I dug out of a drawer and go for a walk along the lakeside. I can't deny how beautiful Scotland is, or the warmth it brings to my heart.

I take the path down by the lake towards my old neighbour's house. I wasn't close to Lisa, but she has a beautiful garden. It was sad when her husband died a few years back. I wonder if she's remarried, or is in need of some company. As I get closer, I can see Freddie's truck on the drive. Freddie and Lisa are talking a few metres farther into the garden. I duck behind a bush, hoping not to be seen. *Is he doing work for her, or is this a social visit?*

I can't hear them, but Lisa looks awfully flirty, and Freddie doesn't move away. I scowl, hating that she has her hands on him. I don't usually hide away from confrontation, but I'm not sure if I have a right to be mad she's moving in on my husband.

I watch them for a few more minutes before retreating back to the lodge. Even though it's selfish, I hadn't considered Freddie finding someone else. He's a good-looking man with his dark brown beard and muscular arms from cutting down trees, but I've never had a reason to be jealous before. We'd dated since I first became interested in the opposite sex. While we were dating, he only had eyes for me. The green-eyed monster boils within me, which fills my thoughts with hate, regret, and envy.

When I started working at a local hotel, I never thought I'd be so good at my job. Assistant manager changed into duty manager. I was ambitious, and the hours became longer. Freddie wasn't supportive of my big dreams, and the more time we spent apart, the bigger the wedge between us felt. I thought our love would stay strong, but he withdrew further as I climbed the career ladder. When I was offered the chance to work in Edinburgh, I should have fought harder to keep him. I should've told him I wanted his support. I've been gone for over a year and I didn't expect to feel so much regret, but it's probably too late to tell him what I wanted all those years ago.

I enter the lodge and throw myself down on the bed. I shouldn't be so affected by the idea of him moving on. He wasn't even kissing her. I knew it was going to be hard coming back to Scotland, but I never expected the feelings I'd buried to be so raw. He's allowed to move on. Isn't that what I've done? I've asked for a divorce, for goodness' sake. If that isn't a nail in the coffin, then what is? Although, after seeing him today, he might not have been waiting at all. Maybe he already thought we were over. *Is he dating Lisa?* I don't like that idea at all. Tears flood down my face and I push them away. I need to pull myself together before I spoil my plan by saying something stupid.

***

By the evening, I've prepared a stew with dumplings and put on a pretty black dress. The slippers I save for my room at the hotel are replaced by ballet pumps, making me feel ready for business. I'm not the woman who cries over men. I'm empowered by my career. That was my choice.

Freddie arrives home just after five, and I plaster on a smile to greet him. "Welcome home. How was your day?" I ask, a little too friendly.

"Same as always. The food smells good."

"Will you be joining me this evening?" The hope in my voice is almost too much. I need to calm my nerves.

"Sure. I'll shower and be right out," he grumbles with little enthusiasm.

He disappears into the bathroom, leaving me to dish up the tea. I light a small red candle I find in the back of the cupboard and take the bowls of food to the table. Once I'm sat down, I watch the seconds tick by on the clock. Listening to Freddie move around, I wait for him. When the door to the bedroom opens, I dip my spoon into the dish to give myself something to do.

He appears in a blue flannel shirt and dark jeans. I smile but continue to eat.

"Thank you," he says, gesturing to the food. He takes the seat opposite me.

"It's no problem." I give a crooked smile.

After a few seconds, he says, "While you're here, I don't expect you to cook and clean."

I finish the food in my mouth. "I thought you wanted me to play the role of your wife?" I'm a little disappointed he seems to have changed his mind.

"This isn't the 1920s. A wife can be more than a domestic." He sounds almost angry.

"I like looking after the lodge."

"Well, it's not something you need to worry about anymore."

I bite my lip before I speak. This might not be my home anymore, but I still care about it. "Your words hurt a little."

He looked me directly in the eye. "I'm not the one giving up."

"I saw you today," I say in a clipped tone.

He frowns. "Saw me what?"

"Flirting with Lisa."

He laughs like I'm being ridiculous. "You have a vivid imagination."

"So you're not dating?" I try not to sound as desperate as I feel.

"Not that it's any of your business, but no."

"And she hasn't made any advances?" I stir my spoon around my bowl while looking into his eyes.

"What do you want from me? My relationship with any female is none of your goddamn business." He stands abruptly.

"Why are you getting so worked up?" I stand up too, gripping the edge of the table.

"You show up here, take over my home, and start judging my life. You have no right!" He waves his arms around like he's outraged.

"I didn't expect to feel the way I do," I shout bitterly. I shouldn't have admitted that, but I'm struggling to keep my feelings bottled up.

He stalks towards me. "Oh, yeah? What feelings would they be?" We stare at each other for a few seconds.

My lips part slightly, but no words come out. Instead of speaking from the heart, I use my head to answer. "Admitting I wish things were different isn't going to change anything."

"As far as I'm concerned, nothing has changed since the last time I saw you." He leans in and kisses me hard on the lips.

My eyes widen with shock. "What just happened?"

Anger, frustration, and lust rage through my thoughts as my mind spins into overdrive. Did I want the kiss? Did I give the signal for him to advance? I'm angry, but I'm not sure it's completely with him. I'm angry at myself for enjoying the kiss.

He kisses me again. "I'll do whatever I like, darling."

"Oh, yeah? Well, so will I." I grab his belt and start to undo it. He kisses me hard again.

This is probably a mistake I'm going to regret, but I can't help myself. I want this. I want him more than anything at this moment, and I can't bring myself to stop.

Once his belt is undone, I unfasten his jeans and yank them down. He tugs at the zip on my dress as he kisses my neck. My body comes to life with a feverish need to touch him everywhere. I lift his t-shirt over his head as he pushes down my straps. Our lips connect and the kisses stay angry. My dress pools at my feet and he starts working on my bra. He isn't gentle with me as he hoists me up onto the kitchen worktop. He pulls down his boxers, letting his erection spring loose. He runs his hands up my leg and cups my sex. I lick my upper lip to stop the moan of pleasure I feel becoming vocal.

"Let it out, Kristie. I don't want you to hold back," Freddie says in a husky voice.

"Don't you think we should stop and talk about this first?" I squeal as his fingers dip inside my panties. It's been over a year since I've been touched.

"We haven't spoken in a long time. Why start now?" He pushes a finger inside me, making my breath hitch.

I should be angry at his dig, but I can't concentrate on anything other than the rapture he's causing. It's been so long since we've done this and I'm struggling to think of a reason for us to stop, never mind argue.

"I'm not on birth control," I say.

He continues to push his fingers in and out of me as he watches me intensely. I'm not good at letting someone else take the lead, but as I reach for his dick, he moves away. His pace increases, fogging my mind with pleasure rather than being able to focus on what's right.

"I'm in charge and taking you bare." He removes his hand and pulls me towards him. His dick rubs against my heat. He gives me a few seconds to object, but I don't, and he pushes inside me. I gasp at the full sensation.

"It's been so long. I haven't been with anyone else," I say. An understanding passes between us.

"For me too. There's only ever been you." Lust washes over his features, and I'm pleased it's because of me.

He begins to fuck me, and I wrap my legs around him. I've missed being intimate with him. I arch my back, trying to grip the counter for support. He isn't gentle with me as he takes what he wants. He puts his hand on my clit and I try to move him away.

"It's too much," I say.

"Lose control, Kristie. Do it with me."

He rubs faster, and I'm losing the battle of what's right and wrong. I nod, and he kisses me a little more gently. His thumb strokes my sensitive area until waves of pleasure take over. My body heats until I feel light-headed. The pleasure builds inside me until I can't take anymore.

"Freddie," I scream as I orgasm. He grunts

and comes a couple of seconds after me.

He kisses me a few more times, pulls his pants back on, and sits back at the table to finish his food.

I clear my throat, but he doesn't look up. Adjusting my underwear, I slip down from the worktop. I quickly clean up in the bathroom and change into my pyjamas. Once I'm refreshed, I join Freddie at the table. The silence is deafening, but I can't find a single thing to say. We have a quiet evening, avoiding the topic we should be discussing and barely making idle chit-chat.

Chapter Six
Freddie

Wednesday

My body clock's set to wake early so I can be cutting down trees as the sun rises. This morning is no exception, but the difference is, I have Kristie snuggled into my side. It's probably out of old habits that she's ended up here, but it stirs something deep within me. I don't want to get out of bed and my dicks already hardening. She snores softly and looks irresistible, even in her sleep mask.

It might be selfish of me, but I'd like to start the day right, and I've missed sex. I stroke her back, moving my hand down over the curve of her ass. When she doesn't push me away, I lick along her collarbone, tasting her sweet scent. That's one of the things I've missed about having her here. Her fruity smell already surrounds the lodge, engulfing it and everything inside. My life isn't complete without Kristie in it, and I'm afraid to lose her all over again. But she's here now, and I have to take the moments I have, even if it's just sex.

I inhale deeply as I reach the crook of her neck. She begins to stir in her sleep, but I continue to explore her body. Touching her curves and taking advantage of her drowsy state already has me aroused. She lifts her mask and unleashes hot kisses on my torso. I'm both surprised and excited she's into this even after my cold treatment last night. Having Kristie is a treat, and I'd never take our chemistry for granted.

"Morning," I say, my voice coming out rough.

"Good morning," she says, eyeing up my erection. She climbs on top of me, straddling my waist. She doesn't seem upset after my dismissive behaviour last night, but Kristie was never good at telling me how she feels. I didn't want to pretend everything was okay just because we were intimate.

"What do you think you're doing?" I ask,

turned on even more by her boldness.

"The term is called a quickie when someone is in a hurry." She holds eye contact.

Without any further warning, she grabs my dick and pushes her already wet pussy down onto it. We both gasp at the sensation. She begins to move up and down, riding my cock. Never in my wildest dreams did I think I'd get this view again. I thrust my hips up towards her, deepening the penetration. I wish I could pause time and keep her here forever.

The anger I felt yesterday doesn't emerge as the pace quickens. Our connection is just as intense, but I keep my feelings suppressed. I fuck her, trying to forget this has to end. I thrust harder and faster, loving the noises she's making. I come quicker than I'd like, but Kristie seems satisfied as she collapses onto my chest.

"That was amazing," she says in between breaths.

"I'm glad you enjoyed yourself." I smile

lazily. I don't want the past to dampen what we have in the moment, so I try to shut out my feelings. I don't want to be angry with her.

"Didn't you?" she asks, sounding vulnerable.

"Of course I did. If only I didn't have to get up."

"You know you could take the day off." She strokes my chest.

"I can't. We're already behind schedule, but I'll see you tonight." I kiss her on the head before reluctantly climbing out of bed. I take a shower, get dressed into my work overalls, and set off to work.

***

Thursday

"Why don't we take a slow walk down by the lake tonight," I say as I remove my work jacket.

Kristie smiles, brushing back her hair. She

looks beautiful in her skater dress and slippers. "I was just about to start tea."

"I'll light the barbeque when we get back and throw on a couple of burgers." I kiss her on the lips while undoing my shirt. Her eyes drift down to my chest and my dick twitches.

"Okay. That sounds nice. I'll just clean up first."

"You look gorgeous the way you are." I kiss her softly and my hand wanders down the curve of her breast onto her hip.

"Why don't we have a bath before that walk?" she says, suggestively biting her lip.

I don't need to be asked twice to get naked with her. Without any hesitation, I lift her dress over her head before capturing her lips once more.

She reaches for the buckle of my trousers. "Hey, slow down. I haven't started the water running yet."

"I'm just so freaking horny around you." She tugs my trousers down as my dick stiffens further.

"You do crazy things to me too." I slip my hand into her knickers and her eyes roll back at the sensation. Using my fingertips, I tease her clit.

"I don't think we're going to make it into the bathroom," she says breathlessly.

"Turn around and put your hands against the fireplace." She does as I ask and I shed the rest of our clothes. The tip of my dick presses up against her entrance while I kiss up her neck.

"Fuck me already."

"You're so needy."

She wiggles her ass back, trying to tease my cock. I grab hold of her hips and push my erection inside her, making her gasp. "Yes."

"You like that, don't you?"

"Yes. Give me more, Freddie."

I push in further until I'm balls deep in her pussy. "You're a bad girl begging for my cock."

She used to like my dirty talking, so

hopefully, she still does.

She tries to turn and look at me, but I thrust into her hard. I put my hands on top of hers, holding her in place as I keep driving my dick in and out, faster and faster. Kristie doesn't like giving up full control but she does it for me. She moans my name but doesn't seem capable of forming a full sentence. There's nothing more satisfying than being inside her. She begins to buckle at the knees, and I pull her close, gripping her with one of my arms across her chest. I lick up her earlobe while continuing to keep my pace. Reaching down, I rub my thumb over her clit. As her arms give way, we end up against the wall next to the fireplace, but I'm not finished yet. The pleasure builds within my balls and I'm almost ready to burst. I increase the friction against her clit until she moans out an orgasm. After a few more hard thrusts, I come inside her, filling her with my seed.

"Fuck, I needed that," I confess between

shallow breaths of air. I pull out and rest my arm against the wall above her head.

She turns to face me and looks at me with her big doe eyes. "We're still going for that walk, right?" She looks vulnerable, like she's expecting me to shut down again.

I give an uneasy laugh. "Yes, of course." That first night I was probably a little harsh to her, but I'm willing to enjoy having her here.

"Good." Her smile lights up her face, and I love seeing her like this. I love seeing her happy.

We take a romantic bath with wine and candles. After dressing, we descend on the beautiful Scottish countryside.

"It's so peaceful here," Kristie says.

"Yes. Do you ever miss it?" I ask, but instantly regret it.

"Of course I do." She reaches for my hand, and I squeeze it.

"What's it like living in a city?"

"Every day brings a new challenge. There's

always something going on." She smiles.

"Do you live near the hotel?"

"I live in it."

"I didn't know you could do that."

"Yes. Shannon, my best friend, and I have ground floor apartments. The company want us on site as much as possible."

"Don't you mind being stuck at work all the time?"

"No. The staff are like my family. The people who've been there for years look after each other. It's nice. I think you'd like them."

I'm both happy and sad she's found something she's passionate about. "It's nice that you have that."

"Come on, Freddie. I know you have that here too, with your work friends and Lisa." I sense a little bitterness when she mentions Lisa's name, but she's right. I do have those things.

"Have you dated anyone since you've left?"

"No. Have you?"

"I already told you I hadn't been with anyone."

"You're such a bloke. You can go out with someone and it not lead to sex."

"I wouldn't want to date or be intimate with anyone else."

We fall into silence, but it's not uncomfortable. There are so many things I want to say, but I don't want to ruin our night. We used to walk along the loch all the time, and it's nice to think of the good times we shared. After we get back to the lodge, I light the barbeque and cook our tea. Kristie sits on the deck watching me, and it feels great having her here.

"The burgers are ready," I say, serving them onto a plate.

"Great. I'm hungry after our walk." She rubs her hands together.

"It's all the exercise you've been doing." I open the bread and add a burger.

Kristie blushes. "Yeah, you have been

keeping me fit."

"I can't help it. You're irresistible."

"I miss our barbeque nights." I pass her a burger on a plate.

"Me too. You remember the first one we had and the bush set on fire?"

"I still think that was your fault," she says before biting into her food.

"I'm not the one who thought we needed as many seats in the garden as possible. I was running out of space, and I didn't think it mattered how close I was to that stupid bush."

She laughs. "A lot of people turned up that night."

"Yeah, they did. It was a really good evening." I bite into my own food.

"Yes. I loved catching up with our old school friends. I loved Benny's fruit kebabs."

"That's because you were a menace with them." Kristie always had a new party game to try.

"What can I say? I like my fruit."

"So do I when I'm eating it off your body."

She blushes. "I smelled of pineapple the next day."

"I used to find it for days." I shake my head. I've never seen so many bugs on the decking. It was like the after party was for them.

"We had some good times. Do you still see Benny?" She smiles but looks a little sad.

"Unfortunately not." I frown but recover quickly.

"Aw that's a shame." We hold eye contact for a few seconds and Kristie is first to look away. She takes another bite of her burger.

"Are you having a good night? How's the burger?"

"Yes. It's been nice, and the barbeque's delicious."

"Good."

We finish the food, lock up, and head to bed. Tonight's felt like old friends catching up rather than just sex. As soon as we're in bed, though, we're instantly all over each other.

***

Friday

The last few days passed in a blur of small talk and sex. We don't talk about the real issues or the future. Instead, I've enjoyed what we had.

My phone rings a little after six in the evening, and Lisa's name appears on the screen. Kristie grabs her plate en route to the sink. "Are you going to answer that?" Kristie asks.

"I don't think I should." I frown, not wanting to ruin the vibe we've had these last few days.

"Maybe she has a baby bird stuck up a tree or something." I told Kristie why I'd been making house calls at Lisa's, although now I'm not sure she's understanding.

"Are you still jealous or something?" I pick

up my plate and follow her.

"No. I think you should take her call." She turns on the hot water tap.

"It's rung off now," I say, looking over to the table.

"You can easily hit redial."

I squeeze washing up liquid into the bowl. "Okay, if you're sure." Lisa might need me, so I don't want to neglect my friend, and I need to remember Kristie's stay is only temporary.

"Yes. How many bubbles are you putting in?" She chokes out a laugh.

"I thought that's why everything looks better since you've arrived. Isn't that your secret?" I'm kind of joking, but there's some truth behind my statement.

"There's no hidden recipe. It's just hard work."

"Does that apply to more than the clean cutlery?" I shouldn't dig, but the closer we get to her leaving, the more I wish she'd change her mind. If only I knew what to do.

"If you mean do I work hard at my job, then yes. I know where to put the effort in."

We've been bottling this conversation up for years, so I guess it had to come out at some point. "It's a shame you didn't give our relationship the same kind of attention, so I guess we weren't worth it."

"I never said that."

"What are we doing, Kristie?" I sigh heavily, wishing this didn't have to turn sour.

"You're going to call your friend back and I'm going to wash up."

"There you go again, avoiding the real problem."

She doesn't answer but starts the task she set out to do. I snatch my phone off the table, angry and frustrated. Like a storm, I rush out of the lodge and select Lisa's contact details.

"Hello," Lisa says when the call connects.

"What do you want?" I rudely ask.

"Why are you being a bawbag?" she bites back.

"Shit. I'm sorry. I've just had an argument with Kristie."

"I have a solution. You could be a good friend and take a break from your blissful marriage."

"Who'd want to hang out with my grouchy self?" I sigh. "She's going to leave me again, isn't she?"

"How should I know? But I'm not going anywhere. I'll help you any way I can. Will you return the favour? I really don't want to go to this speed dating thing alone."

The idea of going sounds like torture, but Kristie's not ready to talk, and the idea of going back into the lodge sounds even worse. It'll only result in an argument which I'd like to avoid. "Why can't you do what normal people do and pick up a guy in the pub or with an app?"

"I don't want herpes."

I laugh. "Who says speed dating is going to be STD free?"

"That's why I need your help. Come with me and we can suss the bad apples out together."

"I can't believe I'm agreeing to this. Fine. Where shall I meet you?"

"At the bingo hall."

I rub my eye. "You owe me for this." I hate that building because it's like stepping back in time. The floor creaks and it smells musty. I shudder at the thought.

"Thank you. I'll see you soon."

"Okay. Bye." I hang up and go back inside to get ready. Once I've changed into a smart t-shirt and added a splash of aftershave, I notice Kristie hovering behind me.

"Hey," I say.

"Where are you going?"

I want to be honest with her since we've been sleeping together. "Lisa wants my moral support at the bingo hall. They're holding a speed dating night."

She smiles, which makes me frown. I want her to tell me not to go because she's changed her mind about leaving, but seeing her so amused means that's not going to happen. "Are you joining in? I can't imagine that being your thing."

"Unless you give me a reason not to go, then yes, I'll be at one of the tables."

Her smile fades. "I know I've been a crappy wife, and I'm sorry for that. You deserve someone who'll put you first. I'm not good at dealing with this kind of situation." She looks up while blinking back tears, but I'm done trying to protect her feelings.

"By situation, do you mean my feelings, or our marriage?"

"Don't be like that, Freddie." She clenches her jaw.

"You've been here for five days and all we've done is slip back into our old ways. We haven't talked at all."

"You haven't talked to me either. You asked me to stay for the week, but I don't know what you want from me. I made myself clear when I arrived."

"Isn't it obvious? I want you to stay! I want my wife back! You could've left. Nobody forced you to sleep at the lodge," I shout.

"You know my career is important to me, but you never showed me you were proud of me. You could've come with me."

"I didn't want you to leave, and you know my life is here. Our family and friends all live in Scotland."

"But you didn't fight hard enough for me! You didn't fight for us!"

Pain fills my chest. Keeping her here was probably a mistake, but I need to think before I say my final goodbye. "I told you I loved you. I asked you not to go. I can't deal with this right now. I need to think. I'm going out. I'll see you when I get home."

Without looking back, I get into my truck and drive to the bingo hall. When I step inside, I'm surprised to see two dozen or so normal-looking people waiting to enjoy the evening.

"I'm glad you made it," Lisa says as she walks over to me.

"You look great," I say, which is the truth. She's put a real effort into her appearances for this evening, not that she doesn't look good normally.

"Didn't Kristie mind you coming tonight?"

"She made it perfectly clear we're over," I say glumly.

"Aw. I'm sorry."

"At least you're not saying I told you so." I force a smile.

"You can start living your new single life, and hopefully I'll gain a wingman." She smiles kindly. At least one of us is optimistic. We fill in the paperwork for the session and I take my seat at lucky table number seven.

The bell rings and my first date sits down at my table. "Hello, I'm Freddie," I say, hoping this isn't going to be the longest three minutes of my life.

"Nice to meet you. I'm Pam. So, what's your

story?" She rests her elbows on the tablecloth.

"Pardon?" I lean back into my chair.

"Well, I'm here hoping to score a one night stand with number eleven." She points in his direction, and I turn to look at him. A guy in a smart suit is at the table.

"He's a lucky guy," I say, not sure what an appropriate response would be. "I'm here to help a friend out so she didn't have to come alone."

"So you're not looking for love, sex, or regret?"

"I've already had enough to last a lifetime."

"Don't tell me you're one of those boring types who'd rather be watching TV on your lonesome." She pretends to fall asleep.

"There's nothing wrong with enjoying your own company." At least it isn't tormenting, like this.

"Until you reach sixty and realise you're going to have to get a cat."

"Why would I buy a cat?" I frown.

"Because no one else will give you the time of day."

"Well, I guess they're the golden years," I say sarcastically.

The bell rings and I plea thanks. My next two dates also have an interest in table eleven, but at least they seem more down to earth. Then Lisa joins me at my table for our three minute speed date.

"Hi," she says.

"Are you enjoying yourself?"

"Erm, some of these people have questionable morals, but I have a few more guys to meet." She crosses her fingers.

"I hear table eleven is a catch," I say, pointing in his direction.

She looks over to the guy in question. "I'll keep an open mind."

"Pam recommended I get a cat."

"Who's Pam?" Her eyebrows pull together.

"The female version of me. She's speed dater number seven."

"Are you going to write her down as a match?" At the end of the session I'm supposed to fill in a form which says whether you'd like to spend more time with any of the attendees. If both members give a positive answer, they get the details of the other person. It's like the slow version of swiping right on an app.

"Hell no." I shake my head.

She smiles a little too brightly. "Aw."

"I think I should be honest with you. Even if Kristie leaves at the end of the week, I still won't be dating. I like our friendship, but there will never be more between us and I won't be looking for someone else. Tonight, I came as your friend because you asked me to and no other reason." I may not be able to tell Kristie how much she holds my heart in her hands, but with Lisa, I want to be straight-talking.

"Ouch." She pouts like she's sulking.

"I'm sorry. I don't want to hurt your feelings, but Kristie will always be the love of my life. I don't want to meet anyone new, and

I'm okay with being a long-term singleton." If I can't have her, I don't want anyone else.

"It's okay. Thank you for telling me your true feelings." It seems she's finally accepted there's no hope for us being anything more than we are now. I'm also coming to terms with my own future. Kristie's going to leave, and I'm going to slip back into my old routine.

At the end of the evening, Lisa gets a date with number eleven, and I head home to sleep on the couch.

Before I settle in for the night, I sign the divorce papers and leave them on the kitchen worktop. There's no point in delaying the inevitable. Even though I don't want my marriage to be over, I'm prepared to let go.

Chapter Seven
Kristie

Saturday

I didn't like the way things went down with Freddie last night, but I don't know how to fix it. When I arrived at the lodge, I should've been more insistent on what I wanted. Scotland was my home, but it isn't anymore. I've made such a mess of everything, and I need to set them straight before I leave for good.

Once I'm dressed, I go looking for him. Last night, I could've handled our fall out better. Lisa's someone I should be thanking for being there for him, not someone I should be getting jealous of. He deserves to be happy, and I should let him move on.

The divorce papers on the kitchen worktop immediately catch my eye, and I walk over to it. When I arrived at the beginning of the week, I rested them against the fireplace; I didn't leave them here. As I inspect them, butterflies begin to jumble in my stomach, making me feel nauseous. He's signed on the dotted line so I can start the divorce procedure. I should be happy, but I want to be sick. This week, I've intentionally tried to be overbearing with my old habits, but I don't think that's why he's signed. Not once has he complained about my wax melts or my home-cooked meals. He might've mentioned how clean I've made the place, but I don't really think he minds. I feel numb, like I'm not sure why I came back to Scotland. I slide down the counter onto the floor, staring at his signature. My thoughts are scrambled with the good memories of our relationship, our bad communication skills when it comes to expressing what we want, and the ugly feelings tainting the love we shared. Could I have made a mistake, or is this for the best?

About half an hour later, the front door opens and closes. Freddie enters the kitchen while I struggle to pull myself together.

"I see you've found the documents," he says

with no emotion, like he's selling an old car or an out of date jumper. He goes to the sink and fills a glass of water. Each step makes my heart sink farther down into my stomach.

"Yes," I say after way too long a pause.

"I'm letting you off the hook. There's no need for you to stay until Sunday. You can leave whenever you're ready." He gulps down the water as a way of dismissing me.

"Is that what you want?" My voice comes out weak. I was so ready to tell him we've had a good week but old feelings were just a lapse in judgement. Now, I realise there might be more to it than that. I strain my neck to look at him, wishing I knew what was going on in his head. I want him to be sad or angry instead of calm and collected.

"I'm doing what I should've done a long time ago. I'm letting you go." He sounds final, and my heart feels like it's shattering into tiny pieces.

"Don't you think we should clear the air

first?" My throat's dry like sandpaper, and my tongue feels heavy in my mouth. I know we'll never be friends, but I'd like us to end on civil terms.

"There's nothing you can say that'll make this any easier, so just leave." He's so matter-of-fact and cold.

"I need to know; why did you make me stay all week?" I'm screaming on the inside for him to show me some kind of affection. *Would I really give everything up for him?*

"I thought maybe I could get you to change your mind, but now I've realised I was fooling myself. You were always going to take the job and there was never anything I could do about it."

"I'm sorry things didn't work out for us." I wouldn't be content here. That's something I already knew. I can't let my heart rule when my head knows it wouldn't be the best thing for me. Foundations Manor is where I belong, but I don't want to give up my husband either. I know I can't have both, although it doesn't mean this is easy.

"I'm sorry too," he says.

I take a deep breath. "Okay. I should pack my things." My voice cracks with every painful word. *If only things could be different.*

"I'll take you to the train station once you're ready." He turns to fill his glass once more.

"Thanks." I offer a small smile when he looks at me, but he doesn't reciprocate. Instead, he gulps down the drink.

This is the right thing for both of us. I like the busy city life and my extended family at the hotel. Living in a remote lodge isn't enough for me. If I'm honest, that's why I took the first city job. I'll never be fully satisfied if I stay here, which wouldn't be right for either of us. I pick myself up from the floor and try to look positive.

I enter the bedroom, listening to fleeing footsteps. The door slams shut, leaving me alone again. Warm tears stream down my face as I neatly fold my clothes into my bag. Once I'm done collecting my things, I take a few minutes to look around. I breathe in deeply, closing my eyes. This is a smell I'd like to bottle and take with me. The outdoors, mixed with warmth and manliness. It's the smell of Freddie.

I dab my face with some cold water and give myself a mental pep talk. This is what I came here to do. Now it's done, so it's time to go. Breathing deeply, I push my worries away. Finally, I'm going back to my busy life, where I don't have time to overthink things or overanalyse every second.

The journey to the train station is a blur. It feels like the last day of school, when I thought my world was ending. Freddie and I would no longer have a reason to meet every day, and I worried we'd grow apart. Little did I know, it wasn't the end of our school days that would separate us. We don't talk in our last few minutes in the truck. I sit looking out the window, fighting back my tears.

The station's platform is crowded with people going about their day. The chatter of friends and arrival announcements block out the thumping beat of my heart. Freddie gives me one final hug before I reluctantly get on the train. It's almost like I'm watching someone else's life play out through my eyes. This is probably going to be the last time Freddie and I are together. There are so many things I wish I'd done differently. In a few seconds, this will be over, and anything I haven't said will remain silent between us. It may be selfish of me, but I can see him through the window. Raising my hand, I touch the glass and mouth, "I'll always love you." He doesn't have time to respond as the train pulls away from the station.

My heart hurts more than ever before, and I sob as I rest back in my seat. I'm no longer angry he didn't try to keep us together. We're two different people who belong miles apart, but that doesn't mean I don't love him. I don't regret spending these last few days with him or realising he'll always be the one for me. We've finally closed the chapter, and it's time to let go, but part of me will always be with him.

Chapter Eight
Freddie

One month later
Sunday

Steak and ale pie with a cold beer is the only way to end a tough week. My little haven is going to be turned into my own personal hell. I have two options, but neither is appealing. I can sell my lodge, or live next to a super bullet train line.

Clicking the red button on the remote, I turn the TV on, ready to watch *Luxury Escapes*. It's almost punishment watching my ex-wife-to-be on the show, but I've been addicted since the first episode. Seeing her navigate the hotel is entertaining, and she does it so well. There doesn't seem to be a dull moment, or at least not on the show.

I dig into my pie and wash it down with the beer while settling into my Sunday night routine. Tonight's episode is about a VIP guest, and watching Kristie get flustered is amusing.

Her face has a permanent red tinge, and I can read her well enough to know she's feeling the pressure.

"Fifty years we've been married," the couple say.

"Congratulations on your golden wedding anniversary. You're very lucky to have each other."

"Yes, we are," the husband says, looking into his wife's eyes.

"Do you have someone special in your life?" the lady says.

"Unfortunately, I don't. I had someone once, but it wasn't meant to be." Kristie smiles sadly.

"I believe fate has a way of rewarding the worthy."

"I like your way of thinking, but the hotel is my life partner."

"As long as you're happy, dear," the man says.

"I am," Kristie says, but she seems

uncomfortable answering these questions. I wonder if she thinks about me. Since that day she left on the train, I've considered going after her a thousand times over, but I've always been too afraid to do it.

I gave the divorce papers back to her to post, but I haven't heard anything yet. It's possible she never filed them, but I don't want to get my hopes up. One question I wished I'd asked was why she chose that moment to turn up on my doorstep. I should've asked what triggered her visit. We never discussed getting divorced before, so did she want to move on, or could there be another reason?

The details of the document I filled in shone a negative light on Kristie. She took all the blame for the breakdown of our marriage, and technically, it was me who filed for divorce, even though I didn't write a cheque.

My phone begins to ring when the adverts start, and it's a number I don't recognise. "Hello," I say, answering the call.

"Mr Butler, how are you doing?" a female voice asks.

"Who is this?"

"Just call me your guiding star," she says with a nervous laugh.

"Is this a hoax? I'm not interested in whatever you're selling."

"No. I'm sorry. Please don't hang up."

"You have five seconds to change my mind."

"Oh, God. I feel like I'm on *Countdown*. If your accent wasn't so manly I might be able to concentrate. Have you heard of the *Luxury Escapes* TV show? Of course you have, although Kristie did say you were a bit of a recluse. Anyway, what I'm trying to say is that the last episode is being filmed tomorrow. It would be so awesome if you could make it."

"You're not making any sense. Who are you and what does this have to do with my ex-wife?"

"Ex-wife?" she asks like she's confused.

"Yes, my ex-wife."

"I think you're mistaken. Kristie never sent the papers."

"And how do you know this?" My pulse beings to race.

"Because I'm her best friend, and I watched her burn them when she got home."

"What!" I don't mean it to come out with so much force, but I'm beginning to get worked up.

"She still loves you, Freddie, but you never showed up at the hotel."

"You're speaking in riddles. Spell it out for me in simple terms," I growl.

"Tomorrow, we're filming the last episode of *Luxury Escapes* at Foundations Manor. It would make an entertaining final if you got off your butt and came here for it. Fight for the woman you love. Show her she doesn't have to be an old,   lonely spinster."

The adverts end and Kristie's face comes back onto the screen. She tucks a strand of hair behind her ear and I look at her. Not as the girl she used to be, but at the woman she's become. Kristie's stubborn and determined. Her ambition drove us apart, but I always knew she loved me. *She still loves me.*

I haven't spoken for so long, I think I make the caller nervous. "Ask her to renew her vows, or at least tell her you love her and you're willing to make some kind of sacrifice for her." She gets louder towards the end of her sentence. When she finishes, there's silence once again while I digest what she's saying.

"Okay," I finally say.

"Okay, you're on your way, or okay, you'll think about it?"

"I'm going to pack a bag and get into my truck."

"Yes!"

"Goodbye."

"Goodbye and good luck."

We hang up and I go to collect a few days' worth of clothes. Once I'm ready, I get in my truck and start the long drive.

Chapter Nine
Kristie

Monday

"Do you know why I've called this meeting, Kristie?" Mr Masters says as he steps into my office.

"Well, it's the last day of filming. I think we've shown the hotel is an experience to be desired, and our flaws add character." The show hasn't been perfect, but our ratings have been good.

"You've done an excellent job, but this final episode needs to be grand. I want fireworks that'll fill our calendar for the next year and beyond."

"I've got a few ideas. The VIP guests were a hit. I was thinking today we could give them a full behind the scenes tour. The vegetable garden is looking great."

"I'm sure you'll figure it out. You haven't let

me down yet." Instead of sitting down, he loops back around to the door. "We'll talk soon."

"Goodbye, Mr Masters." Normally, I'm glad for his departure, but today, I'm unnerved. I don't have a big plan to give the show an extra boost. So far, our natural charms have worked.

Shannon enters my office a few minutes after Mr Masters leaves. I pour us both a coffee from the machine before taking a seat.

"So, what did the big boss man want?"

"Nothing really, other than wanting us to make today's episode even better than the previous ones."

"I have a feeling we have nothing to worry about." She winks at me like she has inside knowledge.

"I'm glad one of us does."

"Come on, where's your optimism? Tomorrow, we get rid of this nosy film crew and we can have our lunch on the grass in full view of the guests." She sips her coffee.

"It'll be nice to be able to stop hiding." I

slump into the chair, exhausted.

"I've never spent so much time in my room."

"At least you don't have to sneak around in your own room. I can't even pass the door or flush the toilet."

She laughs. "You might want to give your room a spruce before we start today."

I narrow my eyes. "Why? What aren't you telling me?"

She takes a bigger drink of her coffee, and I copy, watching her.

"Lend me your room card. I'll do it." She smiles, but it holds a fake lightness. She's definitely up to something.

"It's not my birthday, so what's going on?"

"Can't a girl do something nice for her friend?"

"She can, but I'm suspicious this is something else."

"Just give me the key," she says, giving me a pointed look.

I retrieve it from my pocket and hand it over. I trust she's not going to give it to the film crew or anything crazy like that. "It's almost time to listen to today's episode briefing. Shall we go down to the meeting room?" I ask, finishing my coffee.

Shannon looks out the window. "I think we have a situation first."

I mutter a curse under my breath, getting up from my chair. A difficult guest or employee is not what I need right now. My view of the car park is obscured by a big white tent. "What the hell?" I wasn't told about any marquee.

"So, I guess we should go there first?"

"You're not going to offer to handle it for me?" I have no idea what's going on, but I have a feeling it has something to do with Shannon.

"Nope, but I will hold your hand." She smiles.

I nod. She means metaphorically, so we walk through the halls of the hotel and down the stairs. Our usual chit-chat is replaced by her giddiness, and I can't help feeling nervous.

We head inside the marquee, where we find most of our staff, film crew, and the guests who've featured on *Luxury Escapes*. A round of applause breaks out throughout the tent, which makes me smile. I've enjoyed this week, and although I'd like my privacy back, it's going to be quiet around here once the film crew leaves.

I move farther into the room, noticing a familiar guy in a tux. His back is to me, but I'd recognise him anywhere. My pulse quickens with anticipation. I'm standing next to him before the director signals for us to turn. This must be the big finale the show wanted, but it feels like it's just Freddie and me. Everything else around us is insignificant at this moment.

"What are you doing here?" I ask as he meets my eyes.

"I want a second chance," he says.

"But-" I start, but he cuts me off.

"It's my turn to talk."

"Okay. Then talk." I smile.

"I should've fought harder for you the first time. I should've told you I didn't want to live without you."

"I can't go back to living in the middle of the countryside."

"I'm not asking you to. My home is with you. I'm miserable without you, and I don't want to spend another second living with regret."

My heart feels like it's in my throat. "Would you give up everything for me?"

"My younger self didn't work out what I know now, but the past is the past."

"And what about now? Why are you here, Freddie?"

"I want to be with my wife."

I suck in a breath. "You know I didn't send the papers?"

"Yes. Shannon called me yesterday."

I turn to look at her and she signals that she's the culprit. Everyone is silent, hanging on our every word.

"Guilty," Shannon says, making everyone laugh.

I try to block our audience out again and turn my attention back to Freddie. "Are you moving to Foundations Manor?"

"If that's where you are, then yes."

"And what if I said this isn't what I want?"

Someone in the crowd gasps.

He frowns. "I'm going to fight for you until you send me away."

I nod, and my heart fills with love. "What will you do for work?"

"I could get a job in construction or work in the hotel. Hell, I don't care. None of this matters, only you." He gets down on one knee. "Mrs Butler, I know you love me. Will you renew your vows with me?"

He seems so sure of himself. This is what I've always wanted. I do still love him more than anything. If I'm honest with myself, him not being part of my dream does make it incomplete. I've never wanted anyone but him.

"Yes," I say, and everyone cheers. He lifts me up and spins me around.

Shannon appears at my side with a beautiful white gown, and a vicar appears from the crowd. "We're doing this now?" I say, although it makes sense since they are recording this.

He nods, and Shannon ushers me into a small, cornered off room. "This is so magical," she says.

"Thank you for doing this for me." My eyes fill up with happy tears.

"We have a make-up artist, but don't cry or you'll set me off." She hugs me tightly.

This feels really special to me. Having Freddie and my extended family together is everything I ever wanted.

The service is simple and beautiful. It's an ideal end for the show, but also perfect for me too. Freddie and I would've both chosen a no fuss service, and this is a good compromise. It feels effortless and almost like it had been planned for months.

"You may kiss your wife," the vicar says.

Freddie scoops me up and kisses me passionately. Our audience claps, and we walk through a tunnel of rose petals.

After renewing our vows, we spend a little more time filming some parts for the show. It's a couple of hours before we're left alone.

"So, how long are you staying?" I ask Freddie.

"I meant everything I said. None of it was for show. I'll leave when you tell me you want me to," he says.

"What about the lodge?"

"There's been a plan for a new development nearby, and it's going to affect the lodge, but we can talk about that later. To cut a long story short, I'm considering selling it."

"But you love that lodge."

"I love you more."

"I love you too."

We kiss, and it feels just right. We head into

my hotel room and close the door. I don't know all the details of how this will work, but Freddie turning up is all that matters.

The End

* * *

Discover Jody from Chapter One's story in The Heart of Baker Bay.

The Heart of Baker Bay

Jody

Being fired is not a pleasant experience, although it's something I've become good at. I've had more jobs than most people have in a lifetime. When my gran has an accident, I find myself volunteering to manage her seaside café. I'm the last person anyone should rely on, but for some crazy reason, I'm on my way to save the day. What could possibly go wrong?

Adam

Clover Bay is my home. Keeping my head down and enjoying the simple life is all I want. Jody's temporarily staying in the village to help her grandmother. At first, she seems high maintenance, but it isn't long before I can see through the cracks. I don't want to like her, but there is something about her I can't stay away from.

Can one small village set two hearts free, or will Clover Bay become a distant memory of summer dreams for Jody?

My website for more book information:

https://danielle-jacks-author.mailchimpsites.com/

Newsletter

http://eepurl.com/ht2uJH

Printed in Great Britain
by Amazon